First published 2023 by Walker Books Ltd, 87 Vauxhall Walk, London SE11 5HJ

2 4 6 8 10 9 7 5 3 1

© 2023 Tim Hopgood

The right of Tim Hopgood to be identified as author of this work has been asserted
in accordance with the Copyright, Designs and Patents Act 1988

This book has been typeset in Superclarendon

Printed in China

British Library Cataloguing in Publication Data: a catalogue record
for this book is available from the British Library

ISBN 978-1-5295-0233-6

www.walker.co.uk

For Liz and Grant and
to happy times at the hut!

The Happy Hut

Tim Hopgood

WALKER BOOKS

AND SUBSIDIARIES

LONDON · BOSTON · SYDNEY · AUCKLAND

I don't remember the first time I visited Grandpa Martin's beach hut. I must have been tiny. But I do remember it was yellow.

A bright, vivid, sunshine yellow.

Grandpa said he chose the colour so that it would
look like the sun was always shining on his hut. He called it his
"happy hut" and it's true, the times that my two sisters and I
spent there with him were *very* happy indeed.

Every spring, we climbed the
rocks. Grandpa Martin led the way;
he said he knew the beach like
the back of his hand.

He was probably right because
the backs of his hands were all
wrinkly and looked just like
the beach does when
the tide is out!

If it rained, we dodged the showers. Grandpa Martin didn't own an umbrella. He said a little rain was good for us – it would help us grow!

Every summer, we picnicked on the wooden deck. Grandpa Martin let us make our own sandwiches. He liked cheese and beetroot, but no one else did, not even the seagulls!

When we needed to cool down we paddled in the sea. Grandpa Martin rolled up his trousers to just above his knees. Sometimes he misjudged the waves and got completely soaked.

When things like that happened he always said "flipping fiddlesticks!"

Most afternoons
we played cards.

Grandpa Martin
was very good at
cards. He taught
me how to shuffle
the pack and
showed me how
to win!

And each evening, as the sun went down,
Grandpa Martin would read to us.
If at the end we were still awake, we'd
count the stars together,

until

one by one

we drifted off

to sleep.

We visited in autumn too!
The beach wasn't so
busy then, but it was my
favourite time of year
at the hut.

I remember the
year Grandpa Martin
made us each a kite
and taught us about
the wind and what
different clouds tell us
about the weather.

Autumn was also the time of
year when Grandpa Martin had
to do ESSENTIAL repairs and
repainting, ready for next year.

We all helped. Grandpa called us his Happy Hut Helpers.

He showed us how to use the big saw
and sometimes let me climb the ladder.
But not if it was windy!

In winter, Grandpa Martin always lit the little stove.
He said hot tea and fruit cake were wintertime necessities,
along with woolly socks and tartan slippers.

We often walked along the shore and when we
returned the hut was always waiting for us,
all warm and cosy.

We loved visiting the hut
and the hut loved us being there,
all of us: me, my two sisters, Mum, Dad,
Grandpa Martin and his dog, lovely Tess.

Then one spring, Grandpa Martin wasn't well. He had a bad cough that wouldn't go away. We went to visit him, but we didn't visit the hut.

We didn't visit all summer – Grandpa Martin still wasn't well enough. And in the autumn no one was there to do the essential repairs.

I thought about the hut and how lonely
it must be with no one visiting.

During the following winter when
Grandpa Martin was ill, there was a huge storm
at the beach. It was the biggest storm for years.
Dad told me not to worry about the hut, but I kept
thinking about the giant waves crashing against
its doors and I hoped it was still standing.

When we went the following spring we found the hut
badly battered and in need of urgent repairs. The storm had
moved the beach around, everything was different, and
it felt sad to be there without Grandpa Martin.

We set up a task force. Each of us had a job to do. Mine was to help repaint the hut. We painted it sky blue.

Dad said that way, whatever the weather, there would always be a patch of blue sky on the beach to remind us of Grandpa Martin.

And despite the fact that Grandpa wasn't
there, once all the repairs were completed,
the little hut looked happy once more!
Dad said there was one last thing he needed
to do. We stood and watched as he fixed
a name plate over the doorway.

The sign read "MARTIN", and for a
moment no one said anything ...

... we were too busy remembering
Grandpa and all the happy
memories we'd made
together.

Later on, a shaft of sunlight swept across
the beach and I felt Grandpa Martin was
with us once more, here in ...

our
happy
hut!

To Mum and Dad for all the stories
and to Lou, for always being there for me.

First published in Great Britain in 2017 by Andersen Press Ltd.,
20 Vauxhall Bridge Road, London SW1V 2SA.
Copyright © Robert Starling 2017.
The right of Robert Starling to be identified as the author
and illustrator of this work have been asserted by him in
accordance with the Copyright, Designs and Patents Act, 1988.
All rights reserved.
Printed and bound in China.

First edition.

British Library Cataloguing in Publication Data available.
ISBN 978-1-78344-533-2

ROBERT STARLING

FERGAL IS FUMING!

ANDERSEN PRESS

This is Fergal.
What a nice chap!

He's a friendly little fellow.

But when someone
tells him what to do,
Fergal gets very...

very...

ANGRY.

Like when his dad said,
"Fergal, come down for your tea!"

But Fergal wanted to carry on playing.

And then he said
Fergal had to eat all
his vegetables if he
wanted pudding.

Fergal felt fiery.

"It's **not**

FAIR!"

So Fergal didn't get any pudding,
and he didn't get any tea, either.

Fergal got in a pickle on the football pitch.

YOU'RE IN GOAL!

"... goal."

His fiery temper got Fergal into trouble all over town.

Wherever he went, Fergal just couldn't keep his cool.

Finally his friends had had enough.

"Everyone's ignoring
me, Mum,"
said Fergal.

"It's **not**
FAIR!"

"Well Fergal, dinner is in the bin, Bear's buns are burnt
and no one can play football, and that's not fair."

"We all get fiery," sighed Mum, "but we find a way
to cool down. My trick is to count to ten."

The next day, Fergal felt fiery again.

"That's **not...**"

But then he remembered his mum's trick...

"ONE! TWO! THREE. Four. Five..."

... and he didn't feel so fiery.

It had worked!

Fergal noticed lots of animals had their own way to cool down.

When Crow felt fiery, he told his friends about it.

When Fox felt fiery,

he watched the sunset.

Wolf always found a nice
quiet spot and made a
BIG NOISE!

AWOOOOOOOOOOOOOoooo

Cat lay back and had a really good stretch.

And then there was Hare: whizzing about
stopped her feeling fiery in the first place.

Now Fergal had lots of ways to
cool down, and when he didn't waste
his fire on being angry...

... he found there were much more interesting things to do with it.